Butterfly Meadow

Dazzle's First Day

Come flutter by
Butterfly Meadow!

Butterfly Meadow

Dazzle's First Day

by Olivia Moss
illustrated by Helen Turner

SCHOLASTIC INC.

New York Toronto London Auckland Sydney
Mexico City New Delhi Hong Kong Buenos Aires

To my wonderful sister, Mary. With love always.

With special thanks to Narinder Dhami

ISBN-13: 978-0-545-05456-0
ISBN-10: 0-545-05456-7

12 11 10 9 8 7 6 5 4 3 2 1   8 9 10 11 12 13/0

Printed in the U.S.A.

First printing, June 2008

Contents

CHAPTER ONE

The Brand-New Butterfly

It's time to go, Dazzle said to herself.
Oh, I'm so excited!

She wiggled inside her tiny home.
Slowly, the hard shell of the cocoon
around her began to crack. It was dark
inside the cocoon, but as it split open,
rays of sunshine leaked in, warming her.
Dazzle couldn't wait to escape.

Just a little more! she thought, turning this way and that.

The cocoon burst wide open. Dazzle wriggled out and perched unsteadily on a nearby leaf. She felt all crumpled after her long sleep! Carefully, she spread her brand-new papery wings in the sunshine.

"Hey, I'm *yellow!*" Dazzle cried aloud, admiring her outstretched wings. "I'm a yellow butterfly."

Dazzle blinked at all the bright colors around her. After being inside the tiny, dark cocoon for so long, this new world looked amazing. Above Dazzle was the blue sky, and below her was a green field starred with tiny white and yellow flowers. A narrow stream ran along one side of the field.

That water looks nice, Dazzle thought, slowly batting her wings back and forth. *I wonder who lives there?*

Dazzle had so much to learn. She fluttered her wings backward and forward more quickly. It felt good to stretch out! Maybe it was time to take a trip. . . .

Feeling nervous, Dazzle moved to the edge of the leaf.

It's a long way down to the ground, she murmured to herself. *But here goes!*

Dazzle launched herself off the leaf. She hung in midair, her wings beating frantically. For a second, Dazzle felt herself falling through the air! She gave a little cry of fear as she landed back on the leaf with a bump. She rested for a second, then tried again. This time, she only bounced a little. But she wouldn't give up! Dazzle flapped her wings with long, slow strokes. She hovered in the air, then beat her wings faster and faster and soared toward the sky.

"I did it!" Dazzle cried happily. "I'm flying!"

She felt free, fluttering through the warm air. Dazzle dipped down toward the ground again, but soon realized that she was heading straight for a tree.

"Oh, no!" she gasped.

Dazzle flapped her wings faster. She didn't know what to do! She tried to twist to the side, but that made her wings wobble. She swerved sharply as the tree loomed ahead of her, and managed to dart out of the way at the last minute. Phew!

This flying thing is harder than it looks, Dazzle thought, relieved.

She glanced around. Had anyone seen her mistake? There were no other animals or insects in sight. "Am I the only butterfly here?" she wondered aloud.

Dazzle flew on, more slowly this time. As she floated down near the ground, she spotted something. A tiny insect, much smaller than Dazzle, was marching up the stem of a plant. Behind the insect were three smaller ones. They all looked exactly alike — bright red coats dotted with black spots.

Dazzle wasn't alone, after all!

"Hello!" Dazzle called, hovering above them. "I'm a butterfly. What are *you*?"

"We're ladybugs," the biggest insect called back.

"Ladybugs," Dazzle repeated. "You're pretty. Do you walk everywhere, or can you fly like me?"

"Of course we can fly," said one of the smaller insects. "Our mom taught us how. Look!"

All four ladybugs rose up into the air
and hovered around Dazzle.

"What's a mom?" Dazzle asked,
watching them curiously.

"I'm a mom, and these are my
babies," said the biggest ladybug. "I
brought them into the world and will
take care of them until they grow up."

9

"Where's *your* mom?" asked one of the ladybug children.

"I don't know," Dazzle replied. She couldn't help feeling sad. Where *was* her mom?

"Well, it was nice meeting you," said the mother ladybug. "Come along, kids. Let's go find some lunch."

The ladybugs flew away, leaving Dazzle behind.

CHAPTER TWO

Blackbird Attack!

Dazzle fluttered over to a clump of trees in a corner of the field. Suddenly, she heard a loud flapping behind her. Her wings were knocked from side to side by a powerful breeze. Dazzle spun around.

A blackbird swooped down from the sky! Its yellow beak was wide open, ready to gobble her up. Dazzle gasped

with fright as the blackbird tried to grab
her, snapping its beak. She managed to
dart out of the way, zigzagging as
quickly as she could between the green
leaves of a nearby tree.

Just then, everything went quiet.
Dazzle couldn't hear the flapping of the
blackbird's wings behind her anymore.

With a sigh of relief, she decided that
it must have given up. But as she
fluttered out from behind a large leaf,
the blackbird flew straight at her!

"Help!" Dazzle gasped. The big, scary
bird was so close, Dazzle could see the
red inside of its mouth as it snapped at
her again.

Dazzle ducked behind a tree branch,
but the blackbird followed close behind.
Its bright eyes were fixed on her as she
raced to the treetop.

"Someone, please help!" Dazzle
cried again as the blackbird caught up
with her. She could feel her heart
fluttering, but she had to be brave!
With one quick flick of her wings,
she turned in a circle and flew the
other way.

"I didn't know I could change direction that quickly," Dazzle panted, glancing back.

"Oh, no, the blackbird's behind me again!" The blackbird looked angry as it zoomed toward Dazzle. The butterfly's wings beat so fast that her muscles ached.

She darted across the field. Again, she thought the blackbird had given up. But then she heard the terrible *flap-flap-flap* of its wings close behind her.

"The blackbird's catching up again!" Dazzle cried. "Oh, I *can't* be eaten so soon after coming out of my cocoon."

"Over here!" A small voice rang clearly through the air. "Follow me!"

For a moment, Dazzle thought she was imagining things. Then a small pale-blue butterfly skittered through the air nearby. Dazzle stared at it in amazement. Another butterfly!

"This way!" the butterfly called, swooping toward a hedge at the edge of the field.

Dazzle followed as fast as her wings would take her. The two butterflies zoomed across the field, their wings a colorful blur. Dazzle hadn't even realized that she could fly so fast! She was so close behind the little

butterfly that the blue wings tickled her
nose. Dazzle didn't dare look back again,
but she knew the blackbird was still
behind them. How would they *both*
escape from the hungry bird?

The nearby hedge was full of
wildflowers, but the blue butterfly
headed straight for a big plant covered
with pink blooms. It darted inside the

twisting stems of the plant, and Dazzle followed.

"Watch your wings," the blue butterfly told Dazzle. "These thorns are very sharp."

Dazzle noticed that the plant stems were covered with small, sharp needles.

"This is a rambling rose," the blue butterfly added as they landed on a leaf in the middle of the hedge. "No bird can get past *these* thorns!"

The blackbird hovered just beside the hedge, peering through the tangle. With an angry squawk, it flew off.

Dazzle was saved!

CHAPTER THREE

A New Friend

"Oh, thank you!" Dazzle gasped.
"I just came out of my cocoon today
and I didn't know where to hide. I was
so afraid I would be eaten!"

"Just remember to look for a rambling
rose if you ever need to escape from
hungry birds," the blue butterfly told
Dazzle. Then it flew to the front of the

hedge and peeked out.
"The blackbird's finally
gone. Would you like
to get a drink of
nectar? You must
be thirsty after
all that excitement."

"Oh, yes, please," Dazzle said.

The blue butterfly fluttered neatly
between the thorns and out of the
rosebush again. As Dazzle followed,
she noticed how beautiful
the butterfly's wings
were. They shone
bright blue in the
sunshine.

"Come on, I'll take
you to my favorite

flower," Dazzle's new friend told her, flying ahead.

The two butterflies zoomed along the hedge. Dazzle could see that the little blue butterfly was *much* better at flying than she was. It could spin and turn and skim over the tops of leaves, hardly touching them at all. Dazzle knew she'd have to practice a lot to be as good as *that*. Maybe the blue butterfly would help her. . . .

"Here we are!" The blue butterfly hovered above a sweet-scented climbing plant. It was covered with creamy-yellow flowers, tipped with pink. "This is called a honeysuckle." Dazzle's friend unfurled its long, narrow tongue, dipped it into one of the flowers, and took a long drink. "Try some," the blue butterfly said, twirling happily around Dazzle. "It's delicious."

Dazzle lowered her head inside a flower. She took a sip of the sweet nectar.

"Oh, it *is* delicious," she said with a sigh, and had another sip, then another.

A loud buzzing noise behind her made Dazzle jump. She looked around and saw a yellow-and-black insect flying lazily through the honeysuckle flowers.

"Don't be scared," said the blue butterfly. "It's a bumblebee. They're friendly."

"Hello there," called the bee. It took another sip of nectar, then flew over to them. "Isn't this honeysuckle nice? Have you tried the daisies over there?"

"No, we haven't," the blue butterfly replied. Dazzle was too shy to say

anything, but she smiled at the bee.
"Is the nectar good?" asked the blue
butterfly.

"Delicious!" the bee buzzed.

"The cornflowers are yummy this
year, too," the blue butterfly said. "Have
you tasted them?"

"Not yet," said the bee, "I'll do that
right now!" It waved cheerfully and
floated off toward a clump of bright blue
flowers.

"Come on," the butterfly said to
Dazzle. "Let's go try the daisies."

Dazzle followed her new friend
toward a patch of white flowers with
bright yellow centers.

"You know what?" asked the blue
butterfly, landing on one of the daisies.
"You haven't told me your name yet."

"You haven't told me yours, either," Dazzle said, laughing. "I'm Dazzle."

"And my name is Skipper," said the butterfly, taking a sip of nectar. "I'm a holly blue."

Confused, Dazzle took a drink. "I thought you said your name was Skipper?"

Skipper nodded. "It is," she replied. "But holly blue is the *kind* of butterfly I am. What kind of butterfly are you?"

"I don't know." Dazzle glanced back at her wings. "I'm just a yellow butterfly."

"No one is *just* a butterfly!" Skipper declared. "All of us have a name for the type of butterfly we are."

"So what am I called, then?" asked Dazzle.

"I don't know," Skipper said. "But we can find out."

"How?" Dazzle asked.

Skipper flitted around her, looking excited. "There's a big meadow not far from here," she explained. "*All* the butterflies go there. Sometimes the air is so full of butterflies, you can hardly see the sky."

Dazzle couldn't wait to see it! "It sounds wonderful," she said, sighing.

"It is," Skipper agreed. "And I've seen other butterflies there who look a lot like you, Dazzle!"

"Like *me*?" Dazzle asked. "You mean *yellow* butterflies?"

"Yes," Skipper told her. "I bet they'll be able to tell you what kind of butterfly you are!"

"Oh, I'd love to go to the meadow," Dazzle said eagerly. "Could you tell me how to get there, Skipper?"

"I'll take you myself," Skipper said, grinning.

Dazzle was so happy she whirled up into the air. She was going to meet lots of other butterflies — and find out exactly what kind of butterfly she was!

CHAPTER FOUR

Dazzle's Journey

"Follow me, Dazzle." Skipper darted across the hedge, dancing through the sunbeams. "Let's go to Butterfly Meadow!"

Dazzle followed her new friend. They flitted over the field on the other side of the hedge. The field below was full of huge, strange-looking animals. They

didn't have wings. Instead, they had
large furry heads, big eyes, and long tails
that swished back and forth.

"Oh, what are *those*?" Dazzle gasped,
feeling a tiny bit scared. "They're so big."

One of the animals turned toward her
and said, *Mooooo!*

"They're called cows," Skipper
explained. "Don't worry, they're gentle."

"I didn't know there were so many
other animals in the world," Dazzle
remarked as they fluttered past the cows.
"Now I've met ladybugs and cows."

"Well, butterflies are the best, of
course!" Skipper said. "But there are lots
of other animals. Come and see!"

Skipper led Dazzle over to a patch of
tall grass under a tree. "Can you see

anything down there?" she asked as they
landed on a large leaf.

Dazzle was confused. "No, I can't —"
she began. Then she spotted a cozy nest
of leaves, right in the middle of the grass.
Inside the nest was an animal with
brown spikes, curled into a tight ball.
Three tiny, spiky babies were fast asleep,
cuddled up close to their mother.

"Oh, wow," Dazzle breathed. "What
are they?"

"They're called hedgehogs," Skipper explained.

"Do you think we should wake them up?" Dazzle said. "It's such a nice day, and they're missing all the sunshine!"

"Hedgehogs always sleep during the day," Skipper told her, fluttering off again. "They come out at night to eat."

After taking a last look at the sleeping hedgehogs, Dazzle flew off behind Skipper. She had so much to learn! Dazzle had never dreamed that the world would be such an interesting place. Before she was a butterfly, she was tucked up inside her cozy cocoon. She'd only seen faint colors and heard muffled sounds from there. Now everything was bright and beautiful!

The two new
friends kept flying.
Along the way Skipper
showed Dazzle the spider-
webs strung along the
hedges. They spiraled
outward in lots
of tiny rows,
which caught
the summer
sunlight and
glittered like silver.
"Look, Dazzle!"
Skipper called. She
pointed at the honeybees
buzzing around the
wildflowers,
and the

dragonflies skimming the surface of a
nearby stream. The two butterflies flew
through a pretty little forest full of
bluebells, then out of the cool shade into
the sunlight again.

"We're almost there, Dazzle!" Skipper
said, sounding excited. "There's the
meadow, across the next hedge!"

Dazzle could see a beautiful green
meadow dotted with tall feathery grass,
which swayed in the breeze. Hundreds of

colorful butterflies filled the air! Dazzle could see deep red and emerald green, pale blue and gleaming white, vivid purple and orange and brown.

"The meadow's full of butterflies!" Dazzle cried. She couldn't believe her eyes!

"I told you," said Skipper, grinning and flying ahead.

Dazzle watched her friend dart over the hedge into Butterfly Meadow. She suddenly felt nervous. There were a lot of new butterflies to meet here!

Am I ready for this? she thought.

CHAPTER FIVE

Butterfly Friends

Hundreds of butterflies crisscrossed the meadow. They dipped down to the grass, almost brushing it with their wings.

Dazzle had no idea that there were so many different butterflies in the world! Some were bigger than her, while others were much smaller.

"Oh, Skipper," Dazzle gasped, hurrying to catch up to her friend. "This meadow *is* a special place. I hope I find some other yellow butterflies, like me."

"Let's go look." Skipper skimmed across the grass, and Dazzle followed close behind. *Maybe I'll find my mom here*, Dazzle thought hopefully. But even if

she didn't, she *wasn't* alone in the world. There were hundreds of other butterflies!

Skipper flew straight for a large plant in the middle of the meadow. The plant was covered with lavender-colored flowers. Lots of butterflies were gathering there.

"Hi, Mallow!" Skipper called to a small white butterfly. "Hello, Spot! How are you?"

"Hello," Spot, a red-and-black butterfly, called back. "Your wings look really pretty today." She watched Dazzle curiously as she passed.

Skipper landed and settled on a leaf. Dazzle dipped down to join her, feeling shy as all the other butterflies turned toward them.

"This is Dazzle," said Skipper. "She came out of her cocoon today."

"Good job!" some of the butterflies called. "Pleased to meet you."

"Thank you," said Dazzle, embarrassed by all the attention.

"Dazzle doesn't know what kind of

butterfly she is," Skipper went on. "Can anyone help her, please?"

Dazzle looked hopefully at the other butterflies. They fluttered around her, inspecting her markings.

"I know exactly what Dazzle is," Mallow said at last. "She's a pale clouded yellow!"

"Oh, yes," the other butterflies agreed. "Definitely a pale clouded yellow."

"A pale clouded yellow," Dazzle repeated. "That sounds nice." She turned to the other butterflies again. "But where's my mom?"

The butterflies glanced at one another.

"Dazzle, you don't have a mom," Spot explained. "You came from a cocoon. We all did."

"But the baby ladybugs had a mom," said Dazzle. What did Spot mean?

"Ladybugs are different," Mallow replied. "Butterflies are *special*."

"Another butterfly cared enough to lay the egg that made you, Dazzle," Spot said. "But after that, it was up to you to bring yourself into the world on your own."

"And you did, Dazzle," Skipper pointed out. "You managed to wriggle out of your cocoon all by yourself. You're a very clever butterfly!"

"Yes, very clever!" the other butterflies agreed, fluttering around Dazzle. Dazzle slowly opened and closed her wings. She felt proud of herself. She *was* a clever butterfly! And now, with so many butterfly friends, she would never feel alone.

CHAPTER SIX

Feeling Shy

"You know, we haven't seen a pale clouded yellow like Dazzle here for a while," Mallow announced. "We should have a party tonight to welcome Dazzle to Butterfly Meadow!"

"Mallow loves organizing things," Skipper whispered to Dazzle. "We'll have

a wonderful time. Butterfly parties are always fun!"

"Look, the sun's setting," called Mallow. "Let's fly around the meadow and invite everyone to the party before it gets dark."

The butterflies all rose into the air like a huge, colorful cloud. Then they flew off in all directions. Dazzle glanced at

the sky. It was streaked with pink and
gold, and the sun was slowly sinking
out of sight.

"Come on, Dazzle!" Skipper called.
"We'll find some friends and ask them
if they want to come to the party."

"But I don't know anyone,"
Dazzle replied, feeling shy again.

"You will soon!" Skipper
laughed. She floated down
toward the ground and perched
on the petals of a blue flower.
Dazzle flew down to join her.

"Hello!" Skipper said cheerfully
to a spider, which was spinning a
glistening web between two tall
blades of grass nearby. "We're having
a party tonight. Will you come?"

"Oh, yes, please," the spider replied. "May I bring my family?"

"Of course," Skipper said. "The party's for my friend Dazzle. She just came out of her cocoon today."

Skipper fluttered around Dazzle as the spider grinned at them and continued spinning. "See? Everyone's friendly. Now you invite someone."

Dazzle looked around. She saw a large bee dipping in and out of some bell-shaped purple flowers close by.

"Hello," she called uncertainly.

The bee was buzzing so loudly that it didn't hear her.

"Hello there!" Dazzle said again.

The bee popped out of one of the flowers and buzzed over to Dazzle. It was covered in dusty yellow pollen.

Dazzle realized this was the same bee
she and Skipper had met earlier at the
honeysuckle plant.

"Oh, hello again," the bee said.

"I was wondering if you'd like to
come to the butterflies' party tonight,"
Dazzle said shyly.

"A party?" The bee sounded excited.

"Try and keep me away! I love parties!"
It buzzed around the two butterflies.

"We'll see you later, then," Dazzle
said with a laugh. As the bee dived into
another flower, she turned back to
Skipper. "You were right, Skipper.
Everyone *is* friendly."

Dazzle didn't need to feel shy
anymore. And tonight she was going to
her first party!

CHAPTER SEVEN

Party Time!

Dazzle was beginning to feel more at home as she and Skipper flew around the meadow. They invited everyone they saw to the party. As the sun set, the guests began to gather.

"What happened to the sun?" asked Dazzle as it grew darker. A large pale circle appeared in the sky.

"Don't worry," said Skipper. "It'll be back tomorrow. The moon isn't as bright, but our special guests will light up the evening. Look!"

Dazzle saw some little brown insects with large eyes, crawling through the grass toward them. Three stripes on their bodies glowed yellow-green. They shone in the darkness, lighting up the meadow.

"Hello, butterflies!" called the insect at the front of the line. "We're really looking forward to the party."

"They're called glowworms," Skipper explained, smiling at their new guests.

"How wonderful!"
Dazzle said. "Now
we can see
everything."

"This way,"
called Skipper,
leading the guests toward
one of the hedges. "The best nectar
is over here."

The butterflies and their guests
gathered around the hedge to sip nectar
together. As Dazzle sipped from a
honeysuckle blossom, she heard music
coming from overhead. She looked up.
A group of brown birds perched in a
nearby tree, singing loudly.

"Those birds are nightingales," said
Mallow, who was sipping from the same
blossom. "They always sing at our
parties. They have the sweetest voices of
all the birds in the meadow."

As the nightingales' song grew
louder, the butterflies began fluttering
up into the air.

"Come on, Dazzle," called Skipper. "This is going to be fun!"

Dazzle followed her friend. The butterflies swooped and soared, whirling and turning, rising and falling. Dazzle watched her new friends as Skipper flew in circles above her head, Mallow bobbed up and down, and Spot flitted from side to side.

"We love dancing like this," said Skipper. "You try, Dazzle!"

"Yes, Dazzle!" sang the nightingales. "Let's see you dance!"

Dazzle launched herself into the cloud of butterflies. Her wings were trembling.

"Oh!" she gasped as she almost flew straight into a small brown butterfly. "Sorry!"

"Don't worry about it," said the brown butterfly cheerfully.

But Dazzle felt embarrassed. She turned quickly to the left and almost bumped wings with a big yellow-and-black butterfly.

"Sorry," she said again, hanging her head.

"It's OK," the butterfly replied. "We were all beginners once."

The butterflies began moving away from Dazzle to give her more room. But Dazzle felt silly dancing by herself. She fluttered out of the glowworms' light, into the dark edges of the meadow.

I'll never be as good at flying as the rest of these butterflies, Dazzle thought sadly.

CHAPTER EIGHT

Dazzle's Big Dance

Suddenly, Skipper appeared beside Dazzle.

"Stay close to me, Dazzle," Skipper called. "Now, fly to the left."

Dazzle did as Skipper said.

"And now to the right," Skipper told her. "Fly up high with me, and then swoop back down again, like this."

Dazzle was still nervous, and her
wings were trembling so much, she
couldn't fly very fast. But it was easier
now that she and Skipper were away
from the other butterflies!

"Go right," Skipper called. "Now, left.
Down, and then up."

Dazzle realized that the dance wasn't

so difficult after all. Her wings stopped shaking, and she began to have fun!

"Look at me, Skipper!" Dazzle called happily as she fluttered up and down. "I can do it!"

"Come on, then," Skipper called back. "Let's join the others."

Dazzle danced into the middle of the cloud of butterflies. She swirled and

swooped, skimming over the top of the grass and soaring up toward the white moon. This time, she didn't bump into a single butterfly.

"Wow! Look at Dazzle," said Spot. "She's a wonderful dancer."

"Go, Dazzle!" cried the other butterflies and insects in the meadow. Everyone cheered.

Dazzle soared higher, feeling as though her heart might burst with happiness.

Finally, it was time for the party to end. All the guests said good night and headed for home. The glowworms helped everyone see where they were going.

Tired, but happy, Dazzle floated down to the ground behind Skipper.

What a day, she thought sleepily. It was hard to believe that she'd just come out of her cocoon that morning. So much had happened since then!

"Come on," said Skipper. "I'll show you where I always sleep."

She led Dazzle over to the tall plant in the middle of the meadow. There, the two butterflies tucked themselves underneath one of the large leaves, folding back their wings.

"I hope you enjoyed your first day out of your cocoon, Dazzle," said Skipper.

"Oh, I did!" Dazzle replied. "Thanks to you, Skipper. I hope we'll always be friends."

"Me, too," Skipper said. "Good night, Dazzle."

"Good night," said Dazzle.

I'm so lucky, Dazzle thought. *I had a wonderful first day!*

Dazzle felt herself getting sleepier as the glowworms' lights went out in Butterfly Meadow. Dazzle's first day as a butterfly had been a real adventure. She was sure that tomorrow would hold even more adventures!

"Welcome to Butterfly Meadow, Dazzle," Skipper whispered.

"Thanks, Skipper," Dazzle replied.

She closed her eyes.

Dazzle was home.

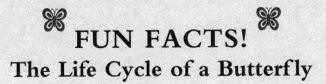

FUN FACTS!
The Life Cycle of a Butterfly

You're growing up. But for a butterfly, growing up means changing *everything*! Butterflies don't start out with beautiful wings. In fact, when they're born, they aren't butterflies at all!

THE EGG

The life cycle of a butterfly begins with an egg. Adult butterflies lay their eggs on plant leaves. But inside these eggs you'll find baby caterpillars, not baby butterflies!

THE CATERPILLAR

Caterpillars are long, worm-like creatures. They are covered in hair and have several sets of legs. Caterpillars must shed their skin to grow! During its lifetime, a caterpillar will increase its body size more than 27,000 times. To grow that big that fast, the caterpillar must spend a lot of time eating!

THE COCOON

When the caterpillar is fully grown, it looks around for the best place to build a cocoon, usually on a plant leaf or stem. The butterfly cocoon is created when the caterpillar sheds its final skin. Inside the cocoon, the caterpillar takes about 10 days to transform into a butterfly.

Butterflies never really "grow up." They emerge from their cocoons at the size they'll always be. Once they are ready, they lay eggs of their own. Then the life cycle begins again!

Dazzle is finally at home in

Butterfly Meadow!

Here's a sneak peek at her next
adventure,

Twinkle
Dives In!

CHAPTER ONE

Twinkle

It was a perfect summer morning in Butterfly Meadow. The deep blue sky overhead was filled with sunshine. Hundreds of colorful butterflies perched on wildflowers, slowly batting their wings back and forth. Others wove their way lazily between the tall blades of grass.

Dazzle unfurled her yellow wings and stretched. She'd slept for a long time, tucked away under a large leaf next to her new friend, Skipper.

"Good morning, Dazzle," said a voice above her. "Let's cool off in the dawn dew before it disappears."

Skipper launched herself off the leaf, and Dazzle followed. The wildflowers and the grass were still covered with cool droplets of dew, sparkling like crystal in the sunlight. The two butterflies skimmed over them, brushing the petals and leaves with their wings.

"Oh, that's nice!" Dazzle sighed, as the dewdrops cooled her down.

"Be careful not to get your wings too wet," Skipper warned her. "Or you won't be able to fly."

The two butterflies rested for a moment on a large, bobbing thistle. Suddenly, Dazzle noticed a beautiful butterfly whizzing across the meadow. All of the butterflies turned to stare as she landed gracefully on a yellow daisy, and she waved her wings in greeting. She was much bigger than either Skipper or Dazzle. Her wings were deep red, with large circles of blue, pale yellow, and dark brown.

"Who's *that*?" Dazzle asked, watching as the big butterfly zigzagged across the meadow, showing off her beautiful wings.

"Oh, it's Twinkle!" Skipper exclaimed as the butterfly fluttered closer.